Other Books by Author
Derek Slaton

Dead Texas Series

1. Day Zero
2. No Comfort
3. Lonesome Road
4. The Journey West

Grindhouse Chronicles Series

1. Smoothen Silky: Demon Fighting Pimp
2. Midget with a Chainsaw
3. Curse of the Blue Diablo (Double Feature with Pestilence A-Go-Go)
4. Smoothen Silky vs The WereCougar

More information can be found at

www.GrindhouseChronicles.com

THE BUTCHER OF CAMP BARLOW

By Derek Slaton

© 2018

PROLOGUE

October 1976

Officer Winston Jones relaxed by the side of the road in his squad car, nursing a warm cup of coffee on a cool fall Texas evening. Much to the displeasure of his fellow comrades in arms, Officer Jones had drawn the coveted Camper's Row beat from the CO, giving him ample time to slack off.

In the entire history of the assignment the biggest problem an officer faced at Camper's Row was a rogue counselor doing a little underage drinking. No robbery, no domestic disputes, no dealing with the drunken fraternity parties on the University of Texas campus.

Just a quiet evening in the country.

The officer perked up when the dispatch radio whined, hoping to hear the troubles his buddies had to deal with that evening.

"Car forty-six, car forty-six, respond."

"Shit," Jones muttered. He picked up the walkie-talkie, shaking his head. *This is supposed to be an easy night, not a working one,* he thought. "Car forty-six." He sighed. "Go ahead, dispatch."

"We got a call from a motorist who saw fireworks coming from Camp Barlow," came the reply.

He sighed again. "Come on dispatch, fireworks? Really?"

"Car forty-six, please be advised we are in the middle of a burn ban, so unless you want to explain to the channel nine news why you ruined thousands of kids camping trips, it would be advisable for you to go get them to cease and desist before they start a wildfire."

Jones paused before responding, dumbfounded by his poor luck. "Ten-four dispatch. Car forty-six en route. Out." He popped the car into drive and headed for the camp.

As the turnoff approached Officer Jones leaned forward in his seat so that get a view of the sky. There were no fireworks, however the sky glowed with the distinctive orange hue of fire.

"Man if I got called out here for a bonfire I'm going to beat the *shit* out of some counselors."

He maneuvered the patrol car along the winding dirt driveway, thick trees creating a darkened hallway for him to drive through. As the forest gave way to an opening, it exposed the source of the colorful sky. Officer Jones looked on in horrified silence at one of the camper's bunkhouses engulfed in flames.

He fumbled for the receiver. "Dispatch, dispatch, I need immediate assistance at Camp Barlow! Fire, EMT, send it all!"

Crackle. "Car forty-six, what is the situation?"

"One of the bunkhouses is on fire, and I don't see the kids anywhere!" he cried.

"Confirmed car forty-six, dispatching fire and rescue now. Do you need backup?"

Jones's eyes focused on a silhouette in the middle of the clearing, a woman laying face down on the ground. He stared at her, praying for movement that never came.

Crackle. "Car forty-six, respond. Do you need backup?"

"Yeah… send… send everybody you can," he stammered, and dropped the receiver. He emerged from the vehicle, approaching the woman on the ground. "Ma'am? Are you okay?" he asked, keeping his head on a swivel. "Ma'am?"

He touched her shoulder, and then hesitated before he flipped her over, hoping that she was just playing an elaborate prank on him.

"Oh dear god," he breathed. Her eyes were seared shut, as if someone had taken a white hot blindfold and strapped it on.

The officer took a moment to compose himself before inspecting her further, leaning over to take her pulse. The light from the fire barely lit her face, so Jones had to feel around her neck for the vein. He quickly pulled back when his fingers brushed a warm, gooey liquid.

He rose to his feet and drew his weapon, hands shaking. Anxiety raced through him as he moved towards the main two story structure that housed the counselors. Lights were on inside, but the lack of movement made him fear for the worst.

Jones readied his service revolver and pushed open the door. It cleared the threshold, but stopped cold six inches later, slamming into a heavy object with a thud. He lowered his shoulder and shoved, forcing the obstacle to scrape across the floor. He gave himself a good two feet of clearance before sliding into the house.

A wave of nausea rolled over him like an avalanche over a hapless skier. His free hand flew to his mouth to prevent his lunch from making a second appearance. Three bodies were strewn across the floor, swimming in a puddle of crimson. Jones remained motionless, mind groping at coherent thought.

"Hahahaha… heheheheheh." The faint sound of laughter snapped the officer snapped back to reality. "Hahahaha… heheheheheh," the voice repeated.

"Hello? I'm a police officer and I'm here to help. Where are you?" Jones asked, straining his ears to get a location on the noise.

"Hahahaha… heheheheheh."

Jones moved slowly through the blood soaked carnage, careful to avoid staining his boots with the blood of the poor teenagers.

"Hahahaha… heheheheheh."

The voice grew clearer the closer he got to the back room. He gently pushed the cracked door, giving a *creak* as it glided open. His eyes glazed over, at the sight behind that door.

A large boy wearing a Camp Barlow Kids t-shirt sat in the middle of the room with his back to the officer. The white wood paneling was splattered with red like it was created by an experimental expressionist painter.

"Hahahahaha… heheheheheheh."
The boy rocked back and forth.

Jones' hand shook as he reached out to the kid. "Son, you need to come with me."

"Hahahahaha… heheheheheheh."

His heart skipped a few beats and he struggled to keep his voice steady. "Son, it's not safe here, we need to…."

The boy turned towards the officer, staring at him with cold dead eyes. "Hahahaha." He cocked his head, pausing mid-laugh to raise his left hand.

His left hand that held the severed head of a male counselor.

Jones immediately turned and ran out of the house, leaving the boy to his own demented actions.

"Hahahaha… heheheheh."

"Hahahaha… heheheheh."

"Hahahaha… heheheheh."

CHAPTER ONE

Ten years later.

Cooper and Pete walked along a tree lined path on the University of Texas campus. October had arrived, but being Texas, the weather was still in the mid-eighties. Perfect weather for the two freshmen to get out and enjoy the coming holiday.

"Come on man, it's a four day weekend, we gotta go do something!" Cooper pleaded, shaking his head. His perfectly styled blonde mullet didn't even move with the motion.

"Your fraternity not throwing a big blowout bash?" Pete teased. "Thought y'all were famous for those?" He poked his muscular companion in the ribs.

"Yeah, they are throwing the party of the year, but since I'm just a freshman I'm not getting an invite," he admitted. "Apparently since the fire marshal shut down the last party we had, the leadership was forced to scale back the guest list."

The shorter boy shrugged. "And freshmen didn't make the cut?"

"Well, I know a lot of freshmen who are going, but they all have tits and like to show them off," Cooper rolled his all-American blue eyes, and then squared his shoulders a bit as a pair of girls strolled across their path. He winked and one of the girls giggled, biting her lip as they walked off.

Pete cracked a smile. The five-foot-five farm boy sure enjoyed riding his good-looking friend's coattails in the babe department. "And I'm sure they do a few other things you are unwilling to do," he continued, and then raised an eyebrow. "At least I *think* you're unwilling."

Cooper attempted to punch Pete's shoulder, just missing as his short friend scampered ahead.

"Mother fucker I will beat your ass!" the blonde bellowed.

"Oh Coop, I didn't know you liked the kinky stuff," Pete mocked, but he didn't get far before Cooper caught his pack and jerked him back.

"Cut that shit out man," he said, eyes narrowed and voice low.

His short friend put up his hands in surrender. "Yo man, chill out. I'm just joking around," he assured him.

Just like that, Cooper pulled out a cigarette and lit it before responding in a much lighter tone, "Come on, let's go meet the girls and talk about what we're gonna do this weekend."

Pete waited for his companion to move on first, not wanting to turn his back on him after the short but intense outburst.

The two freshmen walked up to a picnic table in the middle of the quad and joined two young women. The first, Heather, was a tall buxom blonde with hair so big that there was a hole in a ozone layer directly above her bathroom.

"Ladies ladies ladies, y'all ready for the four day weekend?" Cooper said and threw his arm around her. "Lord knows I am."

The shorter brunette, Daphne, rolled her eyes at the theatrics and leaned in to kiss Pete. "Hi," she whispered, and he smiled fondly at her.

"Hi," he whispered back.

"Hey babe, you find us something to do yet?" Heather asked as she fluttered her eyelashes at Cooper.

He nodded as he ran a finger across the waistband of her jeans. "Oh I know what we're doing, just don't know where we're doing it yet."

"You mean you couldn't get us into your own frat party?" his girlfriend gaped.

"Well, I'm pretty sure he could get *you* an invite if you like," Pete said, prompting an angry glare from his friend. "But I thought it might be fun if the four of us get out of town for a few days."

"We could go to South Padre is-
land?" Heather suggested.

"I'm pretty sure a lot of the
businesses are going to be closed
for the season," Daphne replied.

The blonde crossed her arms and
huffed. "But it's like eighty-five
degrees and I want to go swimming!"

"What about camping? I mean a
lot of these campgrounds have
lakes," Pete suggested.

Heather's eyes lit up. "Oh that
sounds like fun, what do you think
Cooper?"

"Get to see you in a bikini and
check off the woods from our fucket
list?" Her boyfriend grinned. "Hell
yeah!"

"Guys I don't wanna be a party
pooper or anything, but pretty much
all the campsites are going to be
booked up. My dad used to take us

camping a lot and the college break weekends would fill up weeks in advance." Daphne piped up.

"Fuck!" Cooper said and slammed his hand on the table in frustration. "So now what?"

A squeaky voice cut in, "I know a place we can go if you aren't too afraid."

The group looked over see Ritchie, a skinny kid with glasses and faded superhero t-shirt that appeared to be a holdover from his elementary school days. He sat at the table kitty-corner to them, slouched over the latest issue of Omni magazine.

"Bullshit, Ritchie." Cooper waved him off. "You just want to see Heather in a bikini because you're a perverted little cum stain."

Heather smacked Cooper in the arm before leaning in to whisper, "If he knows a place to camp then that little perv can look at me all he wants. Or do you *not* want to check off something from our fucket list?" She pouted.

Cooper bit his lip. "I'm sorry Ritchie, just a little on edge about my biology test. Please, tell us more," he muttered.

"Alright Cooper, I'll forgive you. This time," Ritchie deadpanned, and then trilled a high pitched laugh. "It's a place my granddad used to take me to. It's got a big house, close to the lake, you'll love it."

The blonde couple stared at the brunette couple, and Ritchie bounced on the balls of his feet as they raised their eyebrows at each other with a series of shrugs.

Finally, Pete turned to him. "Yeah, we're in."

"Oh I'll ask Marie to come with us!" Heather gushed.

"If she comes then her boyfriend Edgar will want to come too," Daphne reminded her.

"And her drugged out brother Jake will be attached at her hip too," Pete added.

His girlfriend pursed her lips in thought. "Why *does* he go to every party with her?"

"Pretty sure he's her dealer and it's part of their agreement," he replied.

"Oh," Daphne blinked in surprise.

"So, we're adding three more people to the trip?" Cooper sighed.

Heather tentatively leaned over, strategically brushing her cleavage against his arm. "Do you not want them to come?" She batted her eyes at him.

"Doesn't Edgar's dad own the Beer Barn?" He turned to her.

Heather shrugged. "Um, yeah."

"Then hell yeah they can come," he agreed. "Long weekend at the lake and we have alcohol and drugs covered? Whooo! Fuckin-A man!"

"Again, don't want to be the party pooper, but how are we getting everyone up there?" Daphne spoke up. "Pete's car is in the shop, and we're not all going to fit in mine."

"Well looks like ole Ritchie is going to come to your rescue once again," their nerdy observer said and pulled out a set of keys on a brightly colored keychain. "Cause I got a party van big enough for everybody!" He winked at Heather.

Cooper nearly broke a blood vessel in his head from the stress of holding back his desire to snap the kid in half. Heather blew Ritchie a kiss in return, while rubbing her boyfriend's leg under the table to remind him how they were getting their holiday trip.

Ritchie pounced from his seat and over to her side. "I'm going to gas up your chariot m'lady. Pick you up at your place in an hour?"

"Sounds good tiger, see you then," she replied with a sultry wink, and he scurried off with a spring in his step.

"What the fuck was that?" Cooper demanded, prompting Heather to slide her hand over the zipper of his jeans.

"*That* was getting him to pay for gas instead of asking us to chip in. As well as making sure our fuck-et list gets a little shorter," she licked her lips, and he practically melted beneath her talented hand as it slipped inside his pants.

Daphne cleared her throat and shot to her feet. "So Pete, you want to come help me pack for our trip?"

"Yeah, that's probably a good idea since I'm pretty sure a public jerking is on their fucket list," he replied, laughing as he led her away from the couple.

CHAPTER TWO

"Marie, you guys ready to go?" Heather yelled from the foot of the wood paneled stairs, Cooper draped all over her.

Marie glided down the stairs like a debutante making her social debut. "Yeah, we're coming," she said with a flip of her jet black hair.

"Damn baby, you know we're only going away for the weekend, right?" her boyfriend, Edgar asked as he struggled with three suitcases. "Do you really need all this?"

Marie stopped and pivoted to face him. "Well... if you like, we can leave this one behind," she said and opened the top of the biggest case.

He took a nice long look at what his girlfriend had packed. "Nah baby, this is definitely coming with us," he conceded.

"Hey girl," Marie greeted her roommate. "When's Daphne picking us up?"

"Yeah, about that. Since there's so many of us, we're kinda letting Ritchie drive us," Heather replied.

The ebony haired girl wrinkled her nose. "Why did you invite that perv? He always stares at my ass when I walk by him in chem class."

"Because he has a party van and we need the room so we all can go," Heather said. "Also, it's his grand-father's cabin or something."

Marie pursed her lips. "Well if he stares at my ass, I'm going to smack the shit out of him."

"Just make sure you do it after we're there," Cooper cut in. "Cause we're checking off some of our fuck-et list this weekend and don't want to piss him off." He gyrated his hips suggestively and his girlfriend giggled.

"That's fine as long as doing it our bed isn't on your list," Marie said.

Cooper winked. "It's not anymore."

"Eww!" Marie whined, and then stormed outside in a huff.

"I swear I washed your sheets afterwords!" Heather called as she gave chase.

"Officially man, that's not cool," Edgar said, and paused for a beat until the door clicked closed. "Off the record though, my *man*." He extended his arm and the blonde grinned, exchanging a series of intricate hand slaps to celebrate the achievement. "How many more you got on the list?"

"Seventeen," Cooper replied. "Or... thirty-seven of you include the oft-negotiated but never agreed to bring-a-friend addendum."

Edgar raised an eyebrow. "She doesn't even know about the addendum, does she?"

"And it better stay that way," the blonde threatened.

His dark-skinned friend raised his hands in surrender. "You cool in my book man, I got your back."

Cooper nodded, and then took a deep breath. "So look man, something I need to talk to you about."

"Come on now, why you gotta spoil shit?" Edgar complained. "We had a good moment there celebrating your sexual conquests, and now you're about to ask me to steal beer from my old man."

"If it'll clear your conscience, I'm more than happy to steal twenty bucks out of Ritchie's wallet when he's not looking. He's going to be staring at Marie's ass the whole weekend, so we can chalk it up to a peep show fee."

Edgar blinked. "So, let me see if I got all this. You want me to steal beer from my old man and your solution to pay for it all is for me to visually pimp out my girl to some honky perv for twenty bucks?"

Cooper shrugged. "Forty bucks?"

"Done." Edgar clapped him on the shoulder. "Now let's get the fuck outta here."

They headed outside just as
Daphne and Pete unloaded their bags
from the trunk of Daphne's car.

"Hey guys, glad you could make
it," Edgar greeted as he slapped
five with Pete.

"Y'all ready to have some fun?"
The brunette grinned as he grabbed
the final bag from the trunk.

His friend nodded. "Oh yeah,
this is going to be a kickass weekend."

"Hey Marie, your hair is looking real nice," Daphne complimented
as she approached the two girls.
"Wish I could get my hair to do
that."

Heather and Marie looked at
each other, and then back at Daphne.
In unison, they squealed,
"Makeover!"

Daphne took a step back at their enthusiastic outburst. "Sounds...sounds like fun."

The extended blare of a car horn interrupted the small talk. A fourteen foot long black van pulled up to a stop on the curb, proudly displaying an intricately airbrushed shirtless barbarian decapitating several members of a rival tribe. Ritchie killed the motor and stuck his head out of the passenger side window.

"Ladies, your chariot has arrived," he waggled his eyebrows.

"Dude, *this* is your van?" Cooper grimaced.

"I sense your doubt," Ritchie declared, and hopped out of the vehicle. "Allow me to alleviate your fears!" He flung open the panel door, revealing floor to ceiling shag carpeting, bean bag chairs, and two giant coolers in the center.

Edgar nodded, impressed. "Yeah man, once we go by my pop's place and get some refreshments, I think we can make this work."

Cooper shrugged and finally cracked a smile as he helped load in the bags.

"Hey Marie, is your brother Jake not coming with us?" Daphne politely asked. Pete raised an eyebrow at her. "What?" She lowered her voice. "Just because I'm not a fan of drugs, doesn't mean I'm rude enough to make her leave her own brother behind."

"Oh yeah, almost forgot him," Marie replied, and turned to let out an eardrum shattering whistle.

Across the street, a skinny kid with pale skin and bright red eyes emerged from a billowing cloud of smoke next to what looked like the enforcer from a Mexican drug cartel.

"That's my ride homie," Jake said as he gave the Latin gentleman a fist bump. "Thanks for the smoke out!" He brushed his long wavy blonde locks out of his face before hopping over the porch railing with a faded green duffel bag. "I'll hit you up next week when my shit comes in."

The Latin man nodded before taking another long puff off his joint, adding to the fortress of smoke that had recently been broken by his companion.

Jake tossed his duffel bag into the van, but Ritchie put a hand on his arm before he got in after it.

"Hey just so you know, it's nothing personal," he said firmly. "But no smoking in the van."

"It's all good man," Jake drawled, "I got some brownies that will hold me over."

"Alright, everybody in? We ready to go?" Ritchie bellowed, puffing out his chest as he opened the driver's side door. There was a round of impatient affirmative noises, and he smiled as he peeled out.

CHAPTER THREE

"Oh give me a break!" Marie shrieked. "Everybody knows that Poison is so much better than Bon Jovi!"

"Oh please," Heather replied. "Bon Jovi is hotter, their hair is bigger, and they write better songs. Livin' on a Prayer is this generation's Hey Jude."

Marie threw up her hands. "Girl you are fucking crazy! Brett Michaels is the sexiest man alive!"

"Brett Michaels can't hold a candle to Jon Bon Jovi!" the blonde shot back.

Her friend scoffed. "If you put Jon Bon Jovi in Poison, he'd be the fifth sexiest man in the group!"

"Wait, even below Rikki Rockett?" Heather gaped.

Marie paused. "Well, he is a drummer so he has that timing and rhythm down. Not to mention the endurance."

"Yeah, I can totally see your point," the blonde agreed, and they both paused for a moment, eyes glazing over.

"So Daphne, settle this for us, will you?" Marie finally broke the silence. "Who's better? Bon Jovi or Poison?"

"Well, umm," the brunette replied, picking at the hem of her top, "I'm actually kind of partial to Duran Duran."

The girls leaned together.

"You know, that Simon Le Bon is pretty cute," Heather whispered.

Marie nodded. "He has that accent."

"Oh girl that accent can drop my panties so fast they make a dent in the floor!" the blonde squealed, and they laughed in unison.

"Do you have any idea who the hell they're talking about?" Edgar asked from the other side of the van as he nursed his second beer.

"Based on the album covers, they're a bunch of queers who wear women's clothing and makeup." Cooper shrugged. "Although they do have nicer hair than most of the women we have class with. I mean credit where credit is due."

"I'm telling you boys, never underestimate the power of being on stage," Pete declared.

"Pete's right you know," Jake added, startling them from his reclined position on the beanbag chair.

"Oh yeah? How do *you* know?" Cooper snapped.

"Man, I had a gig last year at this little dive bar," the stoner grunted, not even bothering to open his eyes. "I'd play guitar and sing a few nights a week. Nothing fancy, just some cover tunes and shit. Let me tell you man, I did more mounting and dismounting than an Olympic gymnast."

Edgar laughed. "Bullshit."

"Hey Marie?" Jake drawled.

"Whatever he's saying about his musical conquests is a hundred percent accurate. He has the videos to prove it. Please don't ask why I know that," Marie said.

The three men shook their heads, placed their beers between their legs for safekeeping, and gave Jake a round of applause.

"Alright everybody we're about twenty minutes out!" Ritchie yelled from the driver's seat.

"About damn time Ritchie," Cooper snapped.

Heather glared at him. "If I have to flirt with him, then you have to be nice," she hissed.

"So um, yeah man, where you taking us exactly?" her boyfriend asked gently, leaning forward.

"We are going to be spending the weekend at Camp Barlow," he replied.

"Camp Barlow? Are you serious, Ritchie?" Marie squeaked.

Daphne looked around at her suddenly tense friends. "What's Camp Barlow?"

"It was this camp for orphans that's been closed down for a

decade. God only knows the condition it's in," Pete explained.

Edgar grunted. "Dude what the hell man? You're taking us to an abandoned campsite?"

"What's wrong man, you afraid Jason is gonna get you?" Cooper teased.

Edgar scowled at him. "I couldn't care less about some cracka in a mask, I just don't wanna be spending my weekend trespassing in a run down camp."

"Guys, guys, chill," Ritchie spoke up. "Just sit back, drink your beer, and trust me. You're gonna like. If you don't I'll turn around and drive us right back. Deal?"

"You'd better be right Ritchie," Cooper warned. "You'd better be right.".

CHAPTER FOUR

Ritchie turned the van down the dirt driveway, kicking up dust over the shirtless muscular barbarian. Low hanging branches bounced on the top of the vehicle, a byproduct of the years of neglect the property had endured since that gruesome night in the seventies. The occupants held their alcohol tightly as they bounced side to side on their bumpy journey.

"Yeah this really feels like a well maintained property." Cooper rolled his eyes.

Ritchie slammed on the brakes, thrusting everyone forward.

"Alright, we're here!" He declared as he put the van in park. "Give me a second and I'll come around and open the door for you."

There were three dilapidated bunk houses in view as he opened the door. The one to the far left had been completely burned to the ground, while the middle one appeared to be one strong gust of wind away from collapsing.

The most ominous was the final building with the bars on the windows. The front door was triple chained and there was a giant skull painted on the door above the words *YOU ENTER, YOU DIE.*

The group stared blankly for a moment before Cooper stomped towards the open door.

"You little fucking shit!" he snarled. "After I kick your ass, you're gonna drive us home and then I'm going to kick your ass again!"

Ritchie held up his palms. "Calm down, calm down! Pay no attention to that. We're staying over there." He pointed out of their field of vision.

Cooper hopped out of the van and shoved Ritchie aside to see what he was pointing at. As he turned, his gaze softened and he laughed. "Man, you guys gotta see this."

The three couples milled out and joined him in relieved mirth.

"See, what did I tell you guys?" Ritchie beamed. "Great, right?"

The counselor house was in the final stages of a complete revamping. The grounds were perfectly manicured, a brand new fire pit stood a few yards off the front porch, and a new coat of white paint coated the majority of the exterior. The only portion left incomplete was

at the rear of the house where some
scaffolding tower stood.

"Ritchie, it's amazing. How did
you know about this place?" Daphne
asked.

"Well, about eight years ago my
grandaddy picked up this property
cheap at auction," Ritchie explained. "He came of age during pro-
hibition and spent his first working
years apprenticing with his uncle
making moonshine. So after he re-
tired, he decided to relive his glo-
ry days, bought this place and
started distilling again. Guess he
figured that after the incident none
of the locals would really want to
set foot up here, so it was the perfect spot. He passed on a couple
months back and nobody else in the
family is interested in this place,

so I figured it would be great for a
getaway spot."

"What incident?" Daphne furrowed her brow.

Ritchie scratched the back of
his head. "Back in seventy-six there
was a-"

"Oh who cares? We can have story time at the bonfire tonight. I
wanna go swimming!" Marie cut in.

"Yeah, now you're talking
girl," Edgar said as he wrapped her
up in his arms.

"Alright, so let's grab our
bags, get our bathing suits, and
go!" Heather agreed as she moved towards the back of the van, only to
be stopped by her boyfriend.

"Ladies, we're all friends
here," Cooper said with feigned in-
nocence. "Bathing suits are for when

you are amongst strangers. Let's just go with what god gave us."

Marie and Heather glanced at each other for a moment before playful smiles grew on their faces.

"Alright, but you have to give us a five minute head start to the lake," the blonde ran a finger down her boyfriend's chest, and he grinned.

"Lake is down that path about half a mile," Ritchie blurted, scrambling for his watch. "And the clock starts… now!"

"Come on Daphne, let's go!" Marie waved at the brunette.

"No, that's okay," she replied with a nervous laugh. "I'm not a big swimmer."

"Aw, okay Daph," Heather waved. "Boys, we'll see you in a few minutes!" The two giggling girls began their journey.

About ten seconds passed before Cooper spoke up, "Alright that's been about five minutes, right?"

"Damn straight," Edgar replied and dished out a high-five.

"Yeah, time flies when you're having fun," Ritchie added, shoving his watch into his pocket.

"What do you think Edgar?" Cooper crossed his arms, straightening to his full height. "He thinks he can look at our women in the nude?"

Edgar pursed his lips in thought, cocking his head for effect. "That skinny ass white boy *did* do us a solid with the house," he said, "I think he can get a pass this time."

Cooper stepped over to Ritchie and loomed over him. "Okay, you can come, but no swimming. I see your ass, you drown. Got it?"

"Agreed!" Ritchie yelled and bolted for the trail. "Keys are in the ignition, let yourself in!" His voice faded away as he ran.

"Yo, wait up man, those girls will end your life if they see you without us," Edgar called. Ritchie decided that death was worth the risk, his momentum unbroken. Marie's boyfriend sighed before giving chase to the sprinting pervert.

Cooper shrugged. "Well come on Pete, there are some sights to see brother!"

"You go ahead Coop, I'm gonna stay back, get the generator going and see if I can't scare us up a fire." Pete replied.

Cooper responded by miming a whip cracking, and then darted off into the trees.

"Pete, you know you don't have to stay back on my account," Daphne said, a light blush on her cheeks. "I don't mind if you look at them. I mean, I know they have some things that I don't."

Pete froze and turned to her. "Hon, if I wanted to look at plastic tits I'd go buy a Barbie Doll. You have so much more to offer than they do. It was your shy kindness that made me fall for you at first sight, remember?"

"That's what you tell people," she teased as he gently embraced her. "I heard the real reason is that my ass is so tight if you bounced a quarter off of it you'd get back five nickels."

Pete barked a laugh. "Cooper is so romantic."

"I like your compliments better," she admitted.

Pete grinned. "I mean you're dating me, so obviously you're brilliant."

Daphne smiled and plunked her forehead into his chest. He kissed the top of the head, and she giggled. "Okay, what else?"

"Oh let's see, we've already covered that you're brilliant," he replied. "You're a hell of an athlete, playing volleyball on scholarship, no less. I mean unless they created a league for competitive hair primping those girls couldn't hold a candle to your success."

"Given the amount of hairspray they used, keeping them away from an open flame is probably a good idea," she said.

"Look at that, had no idea you were a comedian as well," Pete replied. "You go on to the lake, I'll take care of the stuff here."

She bit her lip. "You sure hon?"

"Yeah," he assured her, "probably a good idea to keep an eye on Ritchie, make sure Cooper doesn't piss him off to the point that he abandons us up here."

"That's probably a good idea, since this was a hotbed of criminal activity. I can't imagine it having phone service," Daphne said and kissed him quickly before she turned and headed down the trail.

Pete stood and admired her as she walked. *Coop isn't wrong about that ass*, he thought.

"Man you got yourself a hell of a lady there."

"Jesus fucking Christ Jake!" Pete screamed as he grabbed his chest, feigning a heart attack. "Where the hell did you come from?"

"Well I really didn't care where we were staying, since I usually end up passing out in random spots anyway," Jake drawled, leaning against the bumper of the van. "The odds of me ending up in my own bed at the end of the night is about the same as me passing a piss test for a job. Or putting in an application for that matter." He paused, trying to remember what he'd been saying. "Oh, anyway, I just chilled in the van while y'all were talking."

Pete recovered from the defibrillation of his heart from Jake startling him. "Hey man, you want to give me a hand with the bags?" he asked.

Jake grinned and shook his head. "Nah man, I think I'm gonna go hit the lake."

"No worries. Just a heads up though, I'm pretty sure your sister is getting ready to go skinny dipping," Pete teased.

"Eh, I've seen worse," Jake replied as he stumbled towards the path.

Pete pulled out the last of the bags and shook his head. "Don't want to know."

CHAPTER FIVE

Ritchie emerged from the woods about the same time Edgar did, both of them stopping dead in their tracks when they took notice of the beauty before them. Heather and Marie stood no more than ten yards away, their porcelain skin radiating in the light from the low hanging sun.

"Enjoy the show," Edgar said and ripped his clothes off before running towards the girls. When they got a glimpse of the nearly naked Edgar, the nubile goddesses screamed and laughed and ran towards the water.

Ritchie stood motionless, mesmerized like a toddler sitting three feet from a television set. His moment of bliss was broken when Cooper popped up behind him and delivered a light cup check.

"Hey now, are you looking at my chick or his dick?" the blonde teased as his victim doubled over from the love tap to his junk. "Nah never mind, there's not a good answer in there for you."

Ritchie's nostrils flared as Cooper stripped down on his way to join the others. Deep down he wanted nothing more than to pick up the nearest rock and crack open the guy's skull. Before that could happen, however, he needed to sit down and recover from the nut shot. As he rocked back and forth and took deep breaths, his anger subsided a bit as he watched the woman of his dreams pop out of the water, giving him an ever so brief glimpse of those luscious Ds.

Daphne got to the end of the trail and took a moment to admire the scenery. Between class and volleyball she hadn't had much of an opportunity to get out and enjoy nature. She wanted to savor the moment.

"Hey Daphne," Ritchie squeaked out, pain still resonating in his body.

"Ritchie, are you okay?" Daphne asked as she sat down next to him. "What happened?"

"That asshole Cooper happened," he groaned, and sat up with a wince. "He hit me in the nuts because I was checking out Heather. I mean, I just don't get it. Why would a beautiful goddess like her want to be with a dick bag like him?"

Daphne struggled to come up with an adequate answer, but the thought of walking home if Ritchie left got her to dig deep. "Well a lot of girls go through a bad boy phase. She's just young and naive, and having a good time. When she gets a little older and a little wiser then she'll go for a nice guy."

"A nice guy like me?" he asked.

"You never know Ritchie, you never know," she replied, and gently patted his shoulder.

"Damn Ritchie, this place kicks ass," Jake said as he stumbled by the duo.

They watched in amusement as he staggered to the short pier that extended a good ten feet off the shore, holding their breath every time it appeared as though he was going to take a header into the lake. He got to the end and was somehow able to find a seat at the edge, plunking his legs into the water and staring straight down into it.

"Hey you look familiar man, where do I know you from?" Jake slurred, smiling at his reflection.

"Say what you will about Jake, but he appears to get some incredible stuff," Ritchie said before focusing his attention back on the foursome in the lake. He hoped to catch another glimpse of his forbidden fruit.

Daphne scanned the lake, admiring the beauty of the setting sun reflecting in the water. As she stared out something caught her attention from the corner of her eye. Turning her head quickly she saw a large figure about seventy yards away peeking out from the tree line.

As she got up, the figure quickly darted out of sight.

"Ritchie, is there anything around here? Anybody live in the area?" she asked, panic in her voice.

Ritchie startled. "Huh? Oh, no we're alone for about ten miles, and honestly probably further than that since the camps in the area are closed for the season."

"I…I just saw someone in the woods." she stammered.

Ritchie only paid half attention to her, still squinting at the glistening bodies in the water. "You just saw a deer, calm down."

"I saw someone looking at us!" Daphne screeched, getting the attention of everyone in the water. "Now are we alone or not?"

Ritchie was taken aback by her mini-freakout. "Daphne it's okay, we really are alone up here."

"Man, what the fuck did you do to her?" Cooper demanded, stepping in between the two.

Ritchie put his hands up. "Nothing man, she just freaked out when she saw a deer!"

"It wasn't a deer, it was a person!" Daphne insisted.

The other three swimmers scrambled to wrap towels around themselves to prevent Ritchie from passing out.

"It's okay Daphne," Heather said, putting her arm around her frazzled friend. "What did you see?"

"I saw a large man down there, he was staring at us from the tree line," the brunette said, pointing at the spot, "then he vanished when he noticed me."

"Hon it's okay, it was probably just a pervert wanting to get a look at the goods," Marie said as she joined them.

"Yeah well, we already got one of *them*," Cooper said as he smacked Ritchie in the back of the head. "Come on, let's get back to the house. Don't worry girl, we'll be all right there."

Daphne nodded as the group gathered their belongings and moved up the trail.

"Hey Jake, come on man, story time at the fire pit!" Marie yelled over her shoulder.

"Dude man, great talking to you. I'll be back a little later and we can keep chatting," Jake said to his reflection as he followed the group. Just before reaching the trail he noticed a large figure staring at him from the tree line. He shook his head before continuing his trek. "Man this really is some good shit."

CHAPTER SIX

Pete stoked the fire, creating a massive blaze that illuminate a twenty foot radius even though the sun hadn't fully set for the evening. He perked up when he heard the group approaching. "It's about time y'all got back. If you stayed any later you would have been finding your way back by moonlight."

"Yo Pete, get over here man," Edgar yelled as soon as he and Cooper came through the trees.

Upon seeing Heather and Marie supporting Daphne, Pete dropped the stick he'd been holding and ran to them. "My god, Daph, are you okay?"

"Yeah, she just got a little freaked out, that's all," Heather said as they handed her off to her boyfriend.

"There was a man in the woods staring at us," she murmured as she wrapped her arms around him.

"It's okay baby, you're safe now. Come on, let's get you warmed up by the fire," Pete said, causing Daphne to stop in her tracks. "Y'all go ahead, we'll be over in a second." He waved at their friends.

"Pete, I wanna go home," she hissed.

He gave her shoulders a reassuring squeeze. "Baby we're okay. There are eight of us here, we're all together in a big house."

Tears pricked the corners of her eyes. "Pete, please!"

"Daphne, we're safe here," he assured her. "You're surrounded by friends, and more importantly, you have me to protect you. Remember, you were brilliant enough to pick me, so you know deep down you picked me for a reason?" He lightly tickled her ribcage, and she cracked a smile. "There's my girl."

"I'm sorry," she sniffed, blinking away her tears. "I didn't mean to freak out there. It's just, ever since my mom…"

"Daphne," he interrupted and gently raised her chin so their gazes met. "You don't have to explain. I understand."

She grasped his collar and drew him in for a kiss.

"Whooo! Get a room you two!" Cooper catcalled from the fire.

The couple's kiss dissolved into laughter and Pete took her hand.

"Come on Daphne," he said, "I'm pretty sure there's a burger and a beer with your name on it."

CHAPTER SEVEN

"Pete, where in the hell did you learn how to grill a burger like this?" Edgar mumbled around a mouthful of cheeseburger. "This is nothing short of amazing."

"My boy Pete there learned at the foot of the master," Cooper declared.

"Oh please man, you don't know how to cook no burger. Hell you can barely make cereal," Edgar scoffed.

"Nah man, not me. Although it is good to know that I'm the first thing you think of when you hear master," Cooper retorted, eliciting a playful middle finger from Edgar. "Pete's daddy had a pretty good sized livestock farm back home. Every Sunday after church they'd

have this big ole cookout for everybody."

"That's right, my dad has this
fifteen foot pit and he'd fill it up
and grill for hours till nobody
could eat another bite. Those were
great days, but football season was
the best though," Pete said.

Cooper nodded. "Oh, you ain't
kidding. Every time we'd win a game
he'd celebrate by smoking a full
pig."

"Didn't that get expensive?"
Daphne asked after swallowing a
mouthful of beer.

Pete chuckled. "Well luckily
for my Pops, the team wasn't very
good."

"Mother fucker I was the quar-
terback!" Cooper shouted.

"Then you should have known just how bad you sucked," Pete teased.

"He's got you there babe," Heather said as she rubbed her boyfriend's shoulder. She could tell he was getting perturbed, and hoped that some caressing would extinguish his short fuse.

"So Ritchie," Edgar said as he popped the top of another beer, "Now that we are all fed and on our way to being sufficiently inebriated, why don't you enlighten us to the history of Camp Barlow?"

"Yeah I haven't heard this, what's the story there Rich?" Cooper asked as he motioned for Edgar to toss him another brew.

"Guys, I don't know if this is a good idea," Pete cut in.

"Babe, it's okay." She squeezed his hand tightly. "I'll be fine, because I know I have you here to protect me." She offered a smile and he kissed her temple affectionately.

"Okay, so is everybody ready for story time?" Ritchie asked, and received grumbles of impatience in return. "Alright, alright, well this story isn't for the faint of heart which is why I wanted to make sure everybody was on board. Jake, did I hear a yes from you?"

Jake lay just outside the circle people, feet propped up on a rock, a hat pulled over his eyes, and a half eaten burger resting gently on his chest. "Just doin my own thing, brother," he said. "You do you, I'm just along for the ride."

"Alrighty then, here we go." Ritchie leaned forward so that the

light from the fire fully illuminated his pasty face. "The year was
nineteen seventy-six, and Camp Barlow was in their fifth year of oper-
ation. The owner and his wife were
really big into fostering children.
It broke their hearts to know that
they couldn't take in all the kids
who needed parents, so they did the
next best thing and started the
camp. This was a place that was ex-
clusive to orphans, so if you had
parents then no summer fun for you."

"Well unless your parents took
you to Disneyland," Cooper cut in.

"Or the movies," Marie added.

"Or the beach," Heather chimed
in.

"Okay, okay, you get the point
about the camp," Ritchie scowled.
"So ten years ago, one of the camp
counselors just snapped. Nobody

knows what caused it, if he was off his meds, or he caught his girlfriend cheating, or if the kids just drove him over the edge."

"I can totally understand how children can drive someone to kill," Heather said.

Marie gaped. "I thought you were studying to be a teacher?"

Heather shrugged. "That's just because I want summers off."

"Ladies, do you mind? I'd like to find out what the crazy cracka did after he snapped," Edgar said.

"How do you know he's a white guy?" Pete raised an eyebrow.

Edgar snorted. "Dude it was Texas in the seventies, if there was even a single white child there they weren't letting a brotha watch them unsupervised."

"Edgar's right, the crazed counselor was a white kid by the name of Andy Carpenter," Ritchie said as he took back control of the conversation. "According to the official police report, just after meal time he went out to the storage shed, grabbed the biggest axe he could find, and paid a visit to the counselors cleaning up in the kitchen. One by one, he hacked them to death. And when the axe stopped working for him he picked up whatever he could. Red hot pokers, butcher knives, you name it. If it could inflict pain, he was putting it to them. And when the final counselor dropped, he turned his attention to the kids."

"Jesus, he killed the kids too?" Edgar grimaced as he downed the rest of his beer in a vain attempt to rid himself of the mental image.

"There were two bunkhouses that had kids," Ritchie continued, "twenty-two children tucked tightly into their beds. Eleven of them went quickly when Andy chained the door shut and set the building on fire. When the kids in the other building heard their friends screaming, they ran outside, only to be met with a gruesome demise.

"All but one. Fourteen year old Buddy Bagwell. This kid was a beast too, over six feet tall and two hundred pounds. Unfortunately his brain broke a few years prior. When he was eleven, his parents were murdered in front of him, and ever since that day he never spoke a word, only laughing creepily when the mood suited him."

"Poor kid," Marie said, eyes wide. "How did he survive? Hide until the cops arrived and took out the killer counselor?"

"No, see, this is where the story gets interesting," Ritchie said as he motioned for Edgar to toss him a beer. His dark-skinned guest was so enthralled with the story that he complied without question. "The first officer on the scene arrived to find the fire raging and everyone in sight a mangled corpse. The only sound he heard was a child laughing. He tracked it to the back room of the house and found Buddy Bagwell, playing with the severed head of Andy Carpenter."

The group, save for Jake, erupted into a chorus of disgusted noises.

Ritchie held up his hands to calm the rabble. "Now, the official story is that Andy Carpenter killed everyone, and that Buddy acted in self defense. But if you ask the original investigators they will swear up and down that Buddy was the one who decimated the camp."

"Wait, why would they cover that up though?" Pete asked.

"They had a lot of respect for the owners of the camp, and they knew if they blamed it on a kid they brought in that it would destroy them both publicly and privately. So they pinned everything on the coun-selor since he had a criminal record and was only on site because the head counselor hired him without the owner's knowledge," Ritchie ex-plained.

"What about Buddy though?" Heather asked. "If he killed all those people then why did they let him go?"

Ritchie leaned forward. "The police had that covered. He was a ward of the state, and given the trauma he had been through and the mental state he was in, they had Buddy committed to the Bastrop Asylum for the mentally insane. Couple of backroom deals later and they knew he'd be locked up for good, especially since nobody was going to come looking for him and demanding his release."

Heather gasped. "Bastrop Asylum? Didn't that place just burn down a few months ago?"

"Right you are my dear, it did burn down. And if you go back and ask the detectives who are in the know, they'll tell you Buddy Bagwell did it so he could come back to the only place he felt like home. Camp Barlow!" Ritchie bellowed with wide eyes, and waved his hands around.

"Dude that's enough," Pete snapped.

"You're not scared, are you, Pete?" the storyteller teased as he rode his brief moment of popularity.

Pete shook his head. "Nah I'm good, it's just time to move on to another story."

"Buddy's gonna get you, Buddy's gonna get you," Ritchie sang. "Hey, maybe that's who Daphne saw down by the river!"

"Excuse me," the brunette whispered as she bolted from her seat. Pete reflexively grabbed her hand before she shook it loose and kept moving. "I'm fine, I just need some water."

Pete stood, shaking his head as she disappeared into the lodge. "You happy now, asshole? The next time I say move on then you move the fuck on, you got it?"

"Dude I'm sorry, I…I didn't mean-" Ritchie stammered.

"Save it, man. Look, she hasn't shared this with a lot of people, but when she was ten her mother was killed by a stalker," Pete explained.

Ritchie slumped to the ground, realizing he fucked up bad.

"She saw the man following them but didn't say anything, so she blames herself for the murder. Seeing whatever she saw in the woods today spooked her good. So everybody, drop the Buddy Bagwell shit, we clear?" Pete glared at the group.

"Yeah man we got it, and if this little shit says anything I'll beat his ass personally," Cooper said as he smacked Ritchie in the back of the head.

The dejected storyteller grunted from the impact.

"Alright, well look, I'm gonna go check on her. So we'll see y'all when you come in," Pete said and left the circle.

"Speaking of that hon, you ready to go have a little fun?" Marie asked as she slid her hand into Edgar's lap.

"Ain't gotta ask me twice," he replied, grabbing her hand and leading her away.

"And on that note we're off to check off a box on our fucket list," Cooper declared.

"It's getting a little cold tonight, so we may have to check something off that can be done indoors," Heather replied.

He winked. "Yeah, I got a couple things that fit the bill."

Ritchie watched as his tormentor ran off to have passionate sweaty sex with his dream girl. To complicate matters, that wasn't even the worst part of his evening. He still had to go apologize to Daphne. But that was going to have to wait because he still had beer.

"Well Jake, looks like it's just you and me," he said.

Jake pulled himself off the ground, his half eaten cheeseburger plummeting to his feet in the process. "Nah sorry man, but I gotta head back down to the lake and finish my conversation from earlier," he slurred as he stumbled off down the moonlit trail. "You have a good night brother, we'll see you tomorrow."

Ritchie toasted himself. "To Ritchie! Hopefully tomorrow is less fucked than today!"

CHAPTER EIGHT

The moonlight illuminated the path to the lake enough that even the doped up teenager could find his way through without landing on his face. Jake stopped just short of the clearing to spark a blunt the size of a baby's arm. He puffed several times to get the ember evenly smoldering.

"Oh yeah… mmmm… goddamn," he croaked as he held the smoke in his lungs. When he exhaled, a massive cloud enveloped him and left a haze hovering at the tree line. "So where's my friend at?" He asked as he stumbled down to the edge of the pier. "There you are!" He kneeled down at the sight of his watery doppelgänger.

His mumbling conversation continued until there was a loud thud
against the wood on the pier. Jake
bolted to his feet and to attention,
a reflex brought on by several en-
counters with cops.

"Hey, I'm good, how are you?"
He blurted, keeping his expression
level.

It took his eyes a moment to
focus, and even when they did he
couldn't fully grasp the sight in
front of him. A giant of a man, six
foot four, three hundred pounds,
dressed in dark and dingy tattered
work clothes that were singed along
the edges. Grimy bandages caked with
dirt encircled his face and arms.

"Whoa man, you're a big dude,"
Jake stammered as he stepped forward, extending his blunt in the
process. "I don't know if you're

gonna feel this or not, but man, you can totally hit it if you want."

The man lifted his right arm a couple feet off the ground, grasping the wooden handle of a rusted pick-axe. As Jake kept walking the mysterious stranger slammed the metal head to the ground, splintering the wood and causing Jake to flinch at the sound.

Despite the Keith Richards level of drugs in his system, Jake sobered up very quickly. "Hey man, I'm, yeah, I'm just gonna ahead and go home. You, you have a great night." He took a deep breath before making his move towards dry land, only to face off with the blunt end of the pickaxe slamming into his chest.

The impact drove the air from his lungs and sent him tumbling to

the pier, landing hard on his back.
As he gasped, his attacker stepped
towards him. He tried to plead for
mercy as he scrambled backwards, but
he could only wheeze.

Jake was finally able to climb
to his feet before reaching the end
of the peer, throwing his hands up
in the universal "please stop" position. His visual pleas fell on blind
eyes.

The hulking beast flung the
pickaxe up, driving the tip up into
the stoner's jaw. With a violent
pull, the bottom portion of Jake's
mouth shattered, splattering teeth
and blood onto the wooden planks.

He gurgled out some pitiful
sounds as the blood from his par-
tially severed tongue flowed down
into his lungs. The grungy savage
raised the pickaxe as high as he

could, towering over his floundering victim.

Jake made one more futile attempt to plead with the sadist before rusted steel pierced his body. The crown of the blade entered through his collarbone at an angle, the force driving it through his internal organs before cracking into his hip bone.

He remained upright for only another moment, legs quivering from the shock. Finally they gave out, sending his shattered teenage body tumbling backwards into a watery grave.

The beast stood at the end of the pier, admiring his handiwork before his lips parted.

"Hehehehehehehe."

CHAPTER NINE

The water kettle whistled like a locomotive rolling through a small town crossing. Pete rushed over to remove it from the heat so that it wouldn't disturb the others. He knew they wouldn't be sleeping, but he didn't want to be blamed for any performance issues they may have.

"Do you want one tea bag or two?" Pete asked Daphne, who was curled up on the couch with a blanket draped over her.

"One's fine," she replied.

He slipped one bag into a mug. "Cream and sugar?"

"Do they even *have* cream and sugar?" she asked.

"Excellent question," he replied as he opened the fridge. "Well, the only thing in the refrigerator are a half dozen bottles of moonshine, let me try the cabinets." Pete opened the cabinets to find them stocked with even more moonshine. "At the moment I can offer you two varieties of moonshine, chilled and room temperature."

"Just the tea will be fine," Daphne said, cracking a small smile at the absurdity of the situation.

He delivered the warm ceramic cup to his woman, who cradled it to protect every drop.

"Thank you for taking care of me Pete. I'm sorry I'm so jittery," she said.

"Hon, you don't have to apologize for anything," he replied, draping his arm around her in the process. She took another sip before leaning in and placing her head on his shoulder.

Their first real moment of peace and quiet since they arrived was broken as Ritchie came inside.

"Hey Daphne, I really want to-"

"Dude, just keep on walking up to your room," Pete snapped. "You've done enough tonight."

"I just want to apologize to her and then I'll leave you two alone," Ritchie protested.

"Pete, it's okay," the brunette assured him as she straightened up.

Their host walked over to the couch and kneeled down beside them. "Daphne, I'm so sorry I upset you. I was just trying to have a little fun and fit in with these guys. I didn't know about your mom, and if I had I wouldn't have told the story."

"You told them about my mom?" Daphne gaped at her boyfriend. "Why would you do that?"

"Because they were worried about you hon, just like I am. And I figured if I told them they'd stop with the Buddy Bagwell crap so you could enjoy the rest of the trip," Pete told her.

Her eyes softened at his reluctant expression and she nodded. "I understand," she said, squeezing his knee in silent thanks. "And Ritchie, it's okay, I know you didn't mean to frighten me."

"And look, if you're not having a good time and want to leave in the morning, I'll take you home whenever you want." Ritchie promised.

"Thank you Ritchie," she said with a kind smile, putting his guilty conscience to rest.

"Alright, I'm gonna go get some rest. I'll see y'all in the morning, okay?"

"Goodnight Ritchie," the couple said in unison. As he disappeared up the stairs Daphne resumed her comfy position against her boyfriend's shoulder.

"I think I just made a mistake," the brunette said suddenly.

Pete furrowed his brow. "How so?"

"Well I just got myself comfortable, and you're going to have to get up in a second to get me more tea," she teased.

"So that's how it is, huh?" He grinned. "You just snap your fingers and I do your bidding?"

"See, I'm not the only brilliant one in this relationship, you picked up on that pretty quick. Besides, you wouldn't have me any other way and you know it." She fluttered her eyelashes.

"Yeah, you got me there," Pete said as he kissed her forehead. "So one tea bag and no moonshine?"

Daphne smiled. "You know me so well.".

CHAPTER TEN

Ritchie got to the top of the stairs, moving quietly down the hall towards his room. The floor was silent, bringing him a bit of relief. The evening had been rough enough without the prospect of having to listen to his nemesis railing the object of his desire.

Luckily the door cooperated by not creaking as it swung open, giving him what he thought was his first break of the night. It was late, and the only thing he wanted to do was crawl into bed to get a good night's rest. Maybe have a dirty dream or two of the milky skinned goddess in the next room.

He plunked himself down onto the bed, resulting in an eardrum-

shattering creak from the rusted
bedsprings.

He immediately tensed in an attempt to prevent any more noise. He
sat motionless for a few long seconds before his fear was realized.

Cooper moaned loudly from the
next room. "Ohhhhh yeah baby, how
you like that?"

"Fuck my life," Ritchie muttered to himself. The squeaking of
the bedsprings, the soft moans of
pleasure from Heather, and the self
boasting from Cooper resonated in
his brain.

Desperately needing a distrac-
tion, Ritchie grabbed a couple of
comic books from his bag and leaned
up against the headboard to read. He
hoped that envisioning himself as a
cape wearing superhero beating down
douchebags like Cooper would keep

his mind from picturing what was going on in the next room.

"Ohhh yeah girl, you like that big dick don't you?" Cooper said, raising his voice with every thrust. "Yeah, you're getting it good!"

As the moans and egotistical boasting grew louder, the skinny nerd threw a Hail Mary and gently knocked on the wall in the hopes that it would shame them into being quiet. Cooper seemed to take this as a challenge, upping the volume and adding banging on the wall to the audible torment.

"Yeah girl take that cock!" he yelled as Heather's moaning reached a crescendo.

Ritchie focused all of his attention on the illustrated pages before him, but to no avail. Every word he read was drowned out by the cock-bag in the next room.

"Hey! Unless you want a third can you keep it down?!" he yelled as he lost his last shred of sanity.

Much to his surprise, the noise from the adjoining bedroom ceased almost immediately. Ritchie wondered if he had impeccable timing, or if Cooper was just taking a moment to figure out how to torment him further.

With the sound of every footstep and the creak of their bedroom door opening, his heart pounded harder in his ears. He feared his punishment for this would be a swift beating; he could only hope for more swift than not.

Knockknockknock.

Ritchie gulped as the quick raps echoed in his room.

Knockknockknock.

Figuring the longer it took him to answer the more trouble he would be in, Ritchie stood up to take his beating like a man. He took a deep breath, and opened the door, ready to receive a pop to the face.

Instead, his mouth dropped open at the creamy skin of his goddess. Heather licked her lips and leaned on the doorframe, accentuating the swell of her breasts practically leaping out of the low cut bodice of her black silk teddy.

"Hey Ritchie," she purred, "I just wanted to come over here and apologize. Cooper may have went a little too far just now, and that wasn't right."

He struggled to verbalize anything other than half gasps, but finally forced out something resem-

bling English. "It's… it's okay.
Hea…Heather."

"Aww, I'm glad you're so for-
giving," she whispered as she leaned
in a little closer. Her fingertip
made contact with his chest and
slowly moved south, lightly drawing
patterns as she descended. "You
know, you're so sweet. I don't know
why I never noticed that before.".

His heart raced faster than a
junkie blowing an entire 8-ball. If
the blood hadn't been rushing from
his brain to elsewhere he might have
realized this was too good to be
true. At the moment, however, the
only thing his mind could do was
prevent him from visibly drooling.

"Ritchie, I'm going to share a
little secret with you. Something
that a lot of girls won't admit."
Heather lowered her voice. "The bad

boys like Cooper only get the girls until a good guy comes along. Once that happens it's only a matter of time before the bad ones are out, and the good ones are in."

Her hand gently caressed the bulge in his pants, causing his body to spasm like it had been hit with a stun gun. She recoiled in disgust when her fingers came into contact with a warm sticky substance.

"Oh my god, did you just fucking *cum*?" she shrieked in horror, and took a step back.

"You bitch," Ritchie muttered as he grabbed his shoes and ran down the stairs, face reddening into almost purple as his blonde unicorn burst into hysterical laughter.

He stormed by Daphne and Pete without breaking stride.

"Ritchie, you okay? Where are you going?" the brunette asked.

"I'm going to the lake," he snapped. "Y'all really need to pick better friends." Ritchie paused by the kitchen door, opened a cabinet and grabbed a big mason jar of moonshine before storming outside.

Daphne and Pete sat in stunned silence, just looking at each other with confusion. Their moment was broken by Heather coming downstairs.

"Heather, what's going on?" Daphne demanded. "Ritchie just ran out of here all upset. Did you do something?"

"Yeah, I kinda embarrassed him," she admitted, a blush creeping up her cheeks.

Daphne pursed her lips. "What did you do to him?"

"It was just a joke that went too far. I was teasing him and he kinda fired off a shot. You know, like in his pants?" she explained.

"You made that little fucker cum?" Cooper yelled as he came down the stairs. "For fuck's sake, you said you were just going to talk dirty to him, not jerk him off!"

"It's not like that Cooper!" Heather cried as he walked by her, brushing off her attempts to grab him.

"Yeah whatever, I'm going out for a smoke. Try not to jerk Pete off while I'm gone," he snapped and slammed the kitchen door with such force that the windows rattled.

"Sorry guys, I gotta go apologize to him or the rest of this trip is going to suck for everybody," Heather said as she scurried up the stairs to get shoes and adequate outdoor clothing.

Pete sighed. "What do you think hon, we take a private vacation next time?"

"I think that's a given, but at the moment I'm more concerned with making it home from this one," Daphne replied.

"Oh don't worry babe, Ritchie's a good kid, and on top of that I think he likes you. He wouldn't have apologized like he did otherwise. So it's unlikely he'd abandon us out here," Pete said as Heather ran through the living room and out the kitchen door. "Those two, however? Yeah they're probably hitchhiking out of here. Us? We're good."

CHAPTER ELEVEN

"That goddamn fucking slut, how could she do that to me?" Cooper muttered as he stormed into the woods. His ego was bruised at the thought of that little pervert getting gratification from his woman. "I swear to fucking Christ I will beat his ass into the ground if he ever tells anybody about Heather getting his rocks off."

There was a small clearing about ten feet off the trail, which was all the seclusion he required. Cooper gently tapped the bottom of his cigarette soft pack, exposing a lone stick. He pulled it out with his mouth, still muttering obscenities to himself, and lit it up. That first long draw calmed him as the nicotine coursed through his body.

"Oh yeah, that's a lot better." He sighed.

"Cooper, is that you?" Heather asked as she slowly worked her way through the brush.

"Your new boyfriend isn't here, why don't you try looking down at the lake," he replied, vicious sarcasm dripping from his tongue.

"Oh come on, don't be like that," she said as she entered the clearing. "And you know, I don't know why you're so upset. It was your idea for me to go out and teach him a lesson."

Cooper huffed. "I wanted you to tease him, not jack him off like he was a cheap-ass trick."

"Baby, I didn't jerk him off," she said and moved closer to him. "In fact, this is all I did."

She gently grazed his nether
region, simultaneously calming Cooper about one feeling and getting his
blood pumping about another.

"How was I supposed to know he
had a hair trigger?" she asked.

He gaped at her. "Seriously,
that's all you did? Just grazed
him?"

"That's it. Just a simple
touch and he popped off faster than
a champagne cork," she assured him.

"Is that a fact? Well, acci-
dent or not…" he paused, taking a
long drag from his cigarette, "still
couldn't hurt for you to apologize."

Heather shot him a playful
pout, taking a step back from him
and smiling like a girl who enjoyed
being in trouble. He responded in
kind with a crooked smile, his lit
cig dangling from the corner of his

mouth. He undid the top button of his jeans and leaned back against a tree.

"Like I said, an apology couldn't hurt," he repeated.

"Mmmmm… looks like our fucket list is going to get a little shorter tonight after all." Heather licked her lips. She moved into position, standing eye to eye with her demanding beau before sinking to her knees.

Cooper took another long drag from his cigarette as the blonde bombshell unzipped his pants. She reached in and grabbed his member which was at attention and ready for action. He exhaled sharply as she took him in her warm mouth.

He grunted with satisfaction as she slowly worked his cock with her expert tongue. When the speed of her

technique never increased, he took
it upon himself to force the issue.
He grabbed the back of her head and
forced it all the way down, thrusting violently. Her throat constrict-
ed around his meat as she gagged and
she braced her hands against his
thighs, pushing back.

"Easy there tiger. We're not
in any hurry," she sputtered, retak-
ing her position in front of him.
"It's my apology, so I want you to
lean back, close your eyes and let
me apologize properly."

Cooper let go of her hair and
caressed her chin. He stared affectionately down at her, and then gave
her a sharp smack across the face.
This only riled her up more, and she
shoved him back against the tree,
taking him deep into her throat once
again.

He leaned back and closed his eyes as instructed, completely unaware that they had an audience.

Jake's killer, the Butcher, stood silently no more than ten feet away at the other side of the clearing. Despite the close proximity, the trees provided a cloak of invisibility around him.

The savage beast watched as Heather's head bobbed up and down like a piston, forceful and in rhythm. He remained fixated on the young couple, as if he'd never been exposed to a sexual act before. The mesmerizing effect quickly wore off, and the killer drew a long machete from its sheath.

With terrifying dexterity the Butcher raced forward, closing the gap between him and his victims in mere seconds. The noise prompted

Cooper to open his eyes with only enough time to let out a partial scream before he struck.

The maniac rammed the machete into the back of Heather's skull with such force that it went through her mouth straight into her boyfriend's dick. Blood sprayed upwards, coating Cooper's chest and face as he convulsed from the pain of his manhood being reduced to chopped meat. The tip of the twenty-two inch blade dug into the tree, joining the young lovers permanently.

Cooper attempted to scream, but the Butcher muffled it with his large hand. The fight in his victim drained as quickly as the blood running down Heather's perky chest. His head slumped forward, allowing the beast to slam it into the tree to

finish him off with one final sick-
ening crack of his skull.

Satisfied with his handiwork,
the Butcher walked back into the
woods, once again giving the lovers
privacy.

CHAPTER TWELVE

"Pete I'm worried," Daphne said as she stared out the window. Ever since the fight between Ritchie and his tormentors, she had been keeping an eye out. "It's been an hour and nobody has come back yet."

"Baby, it's nothing to worry about," Pete assured her, taking a seat beside her. He attempted to pull her close but she shook him off, not wanting to shirk her duty to keep watch. Undeterred, Pete rubbed her shoulders in an attempt to calm her down.

"Something's not right," she said.

"Daphne, let's stop and think about this rationally. Look at what happened to Ritchie tonight. The girl he's crazy about played a cruel

prank on him, and as a result everybody knows he… umm… has no stamina.
Do you really think he's anxious to
see or talk to any of us?"

She crossed her arms. "No, I
guess not," she conceded.

"And besides, did you see that
giant bottle of moonshine he took
with him?" Pete asked. "If he drinks
even a quarter of that we're going
to find him passed out on the pier
spooning a lake trout."

Daphne chuckled at the mental
image. "Okay, so what about Cooper
and Heather?"

"What *about* Cooper and
Heather?" He rolled his eyes. "You
mean you're concerned about two people who spent an entire week coming
up with a fucket list? A fucket
list. Literally a document listing
all of the various places, positions

and techniques they would like to employ when they fuck. And given how they left here, they were a prime candidate for makeup sex. The only thing that would make me worry about them is if they show up here before breakfast. Knowing those two they are going to show the rabbits how it's done."

The brunette pursed her lips. "Have you seen Jake tonight?"

"Hon, he is so quiet we completely forgot he was riding in the same van as us," he pointed out. "I'm sure he's fine too, just out there enjoying nature in more ways than one."

Daphne continued to stare out the window. "I know you're probably right Pete, but I'm just not going to rest well until I know everybody is safe."

He stopped rubbing her shoulders and got up from the couch.

Her gaze finally snapped away from the window. "You're not leaving me are you?"

"Of course not," he assured her. "I'm just going to grab another blanket and get you a pillow. Figure that's going to be more comfortable for you to lean on than that the edge of that couch."

She smiled. "I love you Pete."

"I love you too, hon. I'll be right back," he said and walked across the room to the closet.

Daphne turned back towards the window, just as a large figure was moved across the driveway. Her face drained of color.

"It's him! He's here! He's here!" she screamed.

Pete ran over to her and attempted to look where she was pointing, but the figure had vanished into the woods. "I'm sorry hon, but there's nothing there."

"I swear Pete, it was the same man from the lake today," Daphne gushed as he buried her head in his chest for comfort. "We have to get out of here, we have to get out of here now!"

"What in the hell is going on down here?" Edgar demanded from the staircase.

Marie followed close behind. "Yeah do you have any idea what time it is?"

"Daphne just saw the man from the lake again," Pete explained.

"Oh for fuck's sake girl, you telling me you woke us up because you bought into that little shit's butcher of Camp Barlow story?" Edgar snapped.

"I don't know if it's the same guy or not, but I swear to you, I saw someone at the lake and I just saw them again walking across the driveway. You have to believe me!" Daphne pleaded.

"Hon, you sure it's not just Cooper playing a joke on you?" Marie asked. "I mean it wouldn't be the first time that prick did something like that."

The brunette shook her head. "Unless he grew another foot and gained another hundred pounds it's not him."

"Man, y'all do your white people shit, I'm going back to bed." Edgar waved his hand at her as he turned to go back up the stairs.

"Goddammit I am not making this up!" Daphne shrieked, fists clenched. Everyone froze, even Pete staring at her open-mouthed. A sob tore its way from her throat and her friends practically flew down the stairs to her.

"Okay girl, okay, your boy Edgar is here now," he said in a soothing tone. "Tell me what's going on."

"I just saw the man from the lake walk across the driveway and into the woods," she said, and took a deep breath to steady herself. "Everybody else is missing, and we're trapped here because Ritchie has the keys to the van." She paused. "I'm *not* making this up. I know you may think I'm crazy because of all that stuff with my mother, but I swear, there is a man out there."

"Okay girl, I believe you," Edgar conceded. "This is what we're gonna do. Your man and I are gonna lock this shit down tight. Ain't nobody gonna get in here unless we want them to. Marie here is gonna move into the kitchen and get us some coffee going, and the four of us are going to sit here getting caffeinated until the sun comes up. Once it does, we're gonna find Ritchie and then we're gonna get the fuck up on outta here and never come back. That sound good?"

Daphne wiped a tear from her cheek before nodding in agreement.

"Okay girl, we got you," Edgar said. "Pete, you get the front of the house secure, I'm gonna lock the back then head upstairs to make sure it's locked down. Then-"

A scream from outside interrupted him. The foursome ran to the windows to see what the commotion was. A skinny figure staggered from side to side near the van.

"Heather you're a fucking whore!" Ritchie screamed, and raised the almost empty jar of moonshine to his mouth. He took a deep gulp and then staggered against the vehicle. "I... I can't believe I wasted so many nights dreaming up the things I could do to you! I hope you're enjoying being Cooper's cum dumpster because that's all you'll ever amount to!"

"I know he's pissed, but goddamn that's cold." Edgar remarked as the group made their way to the front door and out to the driveway.

"Yo Ritchie, you alright man?" Pete yelled, prompting Ritchie to emerge from behind the open van door.

"Hey guys, how… how are y'all doin?" Ritchie slurred. "You have… haven't seen that WHORE Heather around have you? I… I don't want her to go to sl… sleep until I look her right in her cold dead eyes and tell… tell her that she's a fucking WHORE."

"Nah man, we haven't seen her around lately," Edgar replied. "Why don't you come inside and we'll find her?"

"Yeah man let… let me just fin-ish up… here and I'll come on in." Ritchie turned back to the van. "Ha, I bet that cumslut Heather hears that a lo… lot… hahaha."

Daphne's eyes widened as she caught the glint of a blade in the darkness. "Ritchie!" She screamed, and she wanted to run to him, but her feet were rooted to the spot.

He turned and saw the Butcher a few feet away from him. It took his booze-addled brain a moment to register that a hulking figure with an axe was threatening him, and that moment cost him too much.

The Butcher snatched his throat with a grimy hand and tossed him into the van door. Ritchie's head collided with the bottom of it with a dull *thud* and he struggled to get back to his feet, vision swimming.

The deranged savage grabbed the top of the open door and shoved it violently, driving it into Ritchie's chest. The quartet winced in unison at the sound of cracking ribs.

Their host gasped for air, but could collect none with his punctured lungs. He slumped down, his head resting on the edge of the doorframe. The Butcher pulled the door wide open in order to reach maximum velocity with the next slam.

Ritchie's face never stood a chance. The metal part of the door sliced through the bridge of his nose like a samurai sword through a wheat stalk. His body seizured on the ground and blood spurted out from the top of his head, coating the door in crimson.

"You mother fucker!" Edgar blurted and took a step towards the van. Marie grasped his arm in fear, holding him back.

The savage turned to stare at them, and the quartet remained mo-

tionless as they waited on their attacker to make the first move.

The wait was a short one as the
axe wielding maniac threw his uten-
sil of death in their direction before sprinting forward. Pete grabbed
Daphne's arm and bolted, with Edgar
and Marie mirroring their movement
in the other direction. The axe hit
the doorframe of the cottage, splintering wood.

"Come on baby we gotta go,"
Edgar pleaded as he dragged the hysterical Marie by the arm. She collapsed to the ground, forcing Edgar
to drag her like a rag doll. "Baby
please, we gotta go!"

The Butcher retrieved his
weapon before turning his attention
towards the slowest targets.

"Shit," Edgar muttered, letting
go of Marie's hand. The fight or

flight debate had been settled by Marie's inability to run, which forced Edgar to prepare for battle. He stood in between his woman and the madman. "Alright motherfucker, let's do this!"

The Butcher swung his axe horizontally, and Edgar deftly ducked under. He moved in tight for a couple of body blows before the beast shoved him back with hulking arms.

"Goddamn you're a tough son of a bitch ain't ya?" He grunted as he focused his fighting stance, his punches doing virtually nothing.

"Baby be careful!" Marie begged, distracting Edgar for the briefest of moments.

The maniac swung his axe down in the moment, and his victim reached up to catch the object with an instinctive hand movement.

Edgar shrieked as the silver blade caught him between the middle and index fingers. The momentum carried it through his hand and halfway into his forearm before slipping out. He spun around and collapsed to his knees, staring at Marie as the upper part of his arm dangled like a split hot dog.

Tears welled up in her eyes they locked fearful gazes. The murdering madman delivered a strike to the top of Edgar's head, cracking his skull wide open.

With her protector gone, Marie finally pulled it together long enough to run for the woods.

The Butcher pried the axe from the top of his latest kill's head before wailing on the lifeless corpse several more times. He laughed gleefully with each spray of blood that splashed about.

"Heheheheheheh!"

Squish.

"Heheheheheheh!"

Squish.

"Heheheheheheh."

CHAPTER THIRTEEN

Pete dragged Daphne down the trail to the lake, trying to put as much distance between them and that axe wielding maniac as possible.

"Pete where are you going?" The brunette cried, hoping for a reply that made any sort of sense.

He continued to pull her along until she'd had enough. She finally ripped her arm free, forcing her boyfriend to stop and grab at her again.

He grunted as she slipped away again. "Daphne, I know you're scared but we have to keep moving."

"And go where?" she demanded. "We're in the middle of nowhere!"

He motioned wildly in the dark. "We're going to get to the other side of the lake then keep going through the woods."

"You heard Ritchie, the closest place is ten miles away and we don't have a clue which direction it's in!" she cried. "The only way we're getting out of here is getting the keys from Ritchie and driving out in the van."

He knew she was right. If they picked the wrong direction then the elements and wildlife could be just as deadly at the savage killer back at the camp.

"Okay, Daphne, you're right," he said. He squinted suddenly, catching a glimpse of what appeared to be an arm in the distance. He stepped cautiously past his girl-friend to investigate, and all the hairs on her neck stood up.

"What is it?" she hissed.

"I think I see someone," he replied, pushing his way through the brush. As he approached the clearing, he realized it was an arm dangling motionless beside a tree. "Cooper, is that you buddy?" he asked, hoping to hear his longtime friend tell him to fuck off because he was getting some.

But no answer came.

Pete grabbed Daphne's hand as they reached the clearing, both of them grimacing at their friends' gruesome demise. Heather's head was still firmly attached to Cooper's crotch as the ground beneath them soaked up their still warm blood.

"Oh my god, that's a horrible way to go," Pete whispered. He stepped up behind Heather. "Baby, I need you to look away."

"What are you doing?" She gasped as he planted his foot into Heather's back and wrapped both hands around the machete that was holding their friends together. She covered her mouth to prevent from retching as the blade grinded against her teeth and skull.

The recently deceased couple collapsed onto one another after Pete retrieved his newfound weapon. He stepped back over to his girl-friend before bending down to pick up Cooper's lighter that was laying beside his corpse.

"If we're going back then we're going to need to be armed," he said as he handed her the lighter. "Here take this, we might need it."

Daphne nodded and pocketed the lighter with shaking hands. "So, what's the plan?"

"We're going to run straight for the van, you're going to check Ritchie's pocket and I'm going to keep watch." Pete replied. "You find the keys, you get in, and you start it up."

She chewed her bottom lip. "What about Edgar and Marie? We can't just leave them behind to die."

Pete was conflicted, as his first priority was to get the woman he loved to safety, not to mention himself. But he knew if he didn't at least try to save the other two then she'd never forgive him.

"Okay, when we're in the van and have it running we'll honk the horn," he suggested. "If they show up, we all get out together. If that maniac shows up we hightail it out of there."

She crossed her arms. "And just leave them behind?"

"We won't be able to help them if we're dead hon. We'll get to a phone and call the police and they'll just hide until help arrives. Easy peasy," he said, in an attempt to comfort her.

Deep down he felt that if they weren't in the van with them there was a good chance they were goners, but he needed her to stay hopeful so they could survive.

Daphne's voice trembled as she spoke. "Pete, I love you-"

"I love you too babe," he replied, cupping her cheek gently. "Now come on, let's get outta here."

CHAPTER FOURTEEN

Marie's eyes were swollen and red, the image of her lover being lobotomized by an axe wielding maniac seared into her memory. Tears streamed down her face as she haphazardly ran down a makeshift path in the woods, stumbling over every exposed root and rock the forest had to offer.

A branch snapped in the distance, freaking out the already traumatized girl. She turned to run faster, but her feet betrayed her. Her foot caught on a branch, sending the brunette beauty tumbling face first into the dirt.

Panic set in as the disturbances in the forest grew louder. She struggled to get to her feet, moving as fast as she could, but it wasn't fast enough.

The Butcher moved into view when she peeked over her shoulder, his bloody axe in tow. Her screams only seemed to make him move faster, like a dinner bell summoning a hungry farmer to the table.

Distracted, Marie never saw the suspicious leaf pile in the middle of the trail, although with her lack of outdoor experience it was unlikely she would have noticed it anyway.

Her foot stamped down in the middle of the pile, rubber meeting metal as she set off a rusted bear trap. The jaws of the device dug deep into her calf muscle, triggering shrieks that echoed through the woods for no one to hear. Searing pain shot through her body, dropping her to one knee.

"Help! Somebody help me!" she cried.

Her attempts to pry the device open were fruitless. It had been designed to capture and hold quarter ton creatures, so a hundred pound girl stood no chance against it. "Please! Anybody!"

The savage towered above her before moving in close to inspect his prey. She continued to cry and plead as he poked around the booby trap.

"Heheheheheheh," he gleefully hissed, sending Marie into a full blown panic attack.

The beast left her side, moving to the tree next to them. Moments later he emerged holding a thick chain with a noose on the end, tossing it over the large limb above them.

"Oh god, oh god, oh god. You don't have to do this!" Marie sobbed, her pleas falling on deaf ears. She attempted to fight against the behemoth as he draped the metallic lariat around her neck.

She continued to beg for mercy as the Butcher yanked forcefully on the chain, rapidly elevating the young woman off the ground. The noose tightened, slowly strangling the life out of her.

As she swung slowly like a pendulum, he raised his axe and swung with all his might.

The bloodied edge impacted just above her hip bone, shredding through her stomach and intestines. The cut would have been a clean one if not for her spine slowing the momentum of the mighty slash. The Butcher watched with delight as

Marie rocked back and forth across the trail, her innards slipping out of her torso.

"Hehehehehehehehe..."

Like a child playing with a new toy, he pushed the disemboweled shell to keep it in motion. The corpse gracefully swung through the air, painting a bright red design on the forest floor. When she slowed the beast pushed her again, but the force of the shove severed the lower half of her body from the top. The Butcher looked on in disappointment as his plaything was irrevocably broken.

He remained fixated until she stopped moving, wanting to get every ounce of enjoyment from her while he could. As the body came to a stop, the Butcher moved back towards the camp with purpose.

"Oh my god, Edgar," Daphne gasped as they surveyed the crumpled body from the head of the trail. "Where's Marie?"

"I don't know hon," Pete replied, but he knew that if Edgar was cut down that Marie virtually no chance at survival. He carefully scanned the area, relieved to see no movement at all. "Okay, I don't see that big bastard, so we gotta move now."

He sprinted towards the van, brandishing the still bloody machete. His girlfriend followed closely behind, keeping her head down to avoid looking at Edgar's body.

"Coast is clear, find the keys Daphne!" Pete instructed, moving between the van and the edge of the woods.

Daphne was hesitant to touch Ritchie's body, even more so now than when he was alive, although it was a close call. She hovered over him, attempting to summon the courage to riffle through his pockets.

"Have you found them yet?" Pete demanded, his eyes fixated on the tree line.

"Not, not yet," Daphne hesitantly replied. She took a deep breath to psych herself up then dove in like a champ. Reaching in to his right pocket she felt cool metal, resulting in panicked excitement. "I feel them!"

Her boyfriend huffed. "Well get them out and let's go!"

She removed the keys from Ritchie's pocket, but as she pulled her jerked towards her. She squeaked and dropped the keys, blood pounding in her ears before she realized what had happened. "Shit, they're attached to him!"

"Can you get them?" Pete barked the question, momentarily breaking his watch on the woods and staring her down.

She turned to snap at him that she was doing the best she could, but her voice came out a terrified squeak at the hulking figure emerging from the tree line. "Look out!"

He looked back in time to see the maniac closing fast on him. He raised the machete to defend himself, but the Butcher's blood coated hand wrapped around his throat. The killer's momentum slammed Pete into

the side of the van, his head rico-
cheting off of the tacky barbarian
airbrushed there. The violent impact
rendered the boy unconscious, and
his blade tumbled to the ground.

Daphne thought she might die of
fright as she stood there and
watched the life being choked out of
the love of her life.

The fallen machete caught her
eye, and without thinking she
crawled underneath Pete's dangling
legs and grabbed the blade. She
quickly rose to her feet and thrust,
driving it a good six inches into
the slayer's gut.

The Butcher let out a primal
scream and dropped his victim to the
ground, arms flailing wildly in response to the pain. He caught Daphne
across the face, sending her tumbling backwards.

As she picked herself up, the Butcher pulled the machete from his gut like it was nothing more than a small splinter. He tossed it aside before beginning pursuit of his final target.

The brunette sprinted towards the house, reaching it well before her injured predator. She slammed the front door shut and threw the lock, hoping that it would be enough to keep him at bay.

An uncomfortable silence fell over the house. No banging on the door, no shattering of glass, just silence. A panicking Daphne quickly ran to the kitchen, grabbing a steak knife off the countertop.

Trembling and terrified, she held the knife out as far as she could, her body jolting in response to every little creaking sound. She began a slow and steady breathing regiment to calm herself down, a technique her high school volleyball coach taught her.

Normally when she employed this it was to steady herself for a big serve, not to help her survive a massacre. After a few moments her hands steadied, but this was short lived.

The front door latch exploded from the force of the Butcher bursting through, using Ritchie's corpse as a battering ram. Daphne froze and watched helplessly as he tossed the lifeless body aside like a child bored with his toy.

Blood from the machete wound pooled around his gut, staining the grungy dark blue shirt just a little darker.

She broke from her stance like a sprinter out of the blocks, hitting the bottom step before the Butcher could react. He quickly followed, squealing with delight at the chase. Daphne reached the landing first, grabbing a book from the shelf.

As the killer approached the top step, she launched the hardcover at him, striking his face and distracting him for a brief moment. Seizing the opportunity, she lunged forward with her blade, impaling her pursuer in the shoulder. He instinctively lurched back at the strike, throwing him off balance. His massive size combined with gravity did the rest.

Skull violently met wood as the Butcher's head crashed into the stairs. His body slid down the remaining steps, coming to rest gently on the first floor.

She remained vigilant, careful to notice any movement from the deranged killer. When none came, she grabbed another book from the shelf and lobbed it in his direction. It bounced off his large blood soaked belly, drawing no reaction.

"Slow and steady Daphne, just like coach taught you." She cautiously moved down the stairs, pausing half a dozen steps from the killer's feet. Not wanting to risk a surprise attack, she leaped over the banister, landing hard on the wooden floor. When she was satisfied the Butcher wasn't disturbed by her actions, she ran over to Ritchie's body.

The impact from the door had further mutilated his carcass, making him even more repulsive than he was in life. Her hesitancy gone, Daphne rolled him over and went straight for the keys. The keyring was attached to a large silver clamp hooked around his belt loop. She struggled to open it before realizing there was a tightening screw that needed to be loosened.

"Could you be any more paranoid Ritchie?" she muttered.

As she freed the keys in triumph and sprung to her feet. Before she could turn towards the door she pitched forward, hitting the cabinets hard. The force of the impact dislodged the keys from her hand and they skittered across the counter.

As she whipped around, a bloody bandaged hand wrapped around her throat.

"Hehehehehehehehe," the Butcher chuckled, happy to have his plaything again.

Daphne swung with everything she could muster, catching the killer in the face.

"Hehehehehehehehe," he continued to laugh, unfazed by her blow.

She threw her fist forward again, catching him directly in the jaw. He didn't get angry, just laughed as he tossed her aside to the ground. As she struggled to get to her feet he picked up the keys and dangled them in front of her like a mother trying to soothe a crying baby. Without warning, he launched them across the house and into the back room.

"Fuck you!" Daphne yelled as she hobbled out the door.

The Butcher yelled, displeased that his toy wasn't playing fetch with him. He pursued her out the front of the house and towards the dilapidated bunkhouse. She vanished into it a few seconds before he could reach it, the door slamming against the frame but not latching.

The interior of the building was in shambles as the fire a decade ago had done a number on it. Charred beams criss crossed the structure, destroyed bed frames were scattered randomly about, and there was a large hole at the base of the side-wall some wildlife had created to find shelter for an evening. The structural integrity of the dwelling had achieved supermodel status, in that a strong gust of wind could knock it completely over.

Breathe, but not loudly...
Daphne thought as she took cover behind some burned out bed frames. Her hiding place was very obvious given the layout of the room, but the last thing she needed was to give the maniac any more help. She tensed up as the door slowly creaked open, footsteps following closely behind.

"Hehehehehehelheh," her opponent laughed, as if he were a child playing hide and seek.

The footsteps grew louder, forcing her hand. She dove towards the hole at the base of the side wall, hoping that she was thin enough to fit through.

The Butcher saw her and immediately darted after her. The fit was tight, but she was able to squeeze the top half of her body through the opening. She screamed as he gripped

her ankle and jerked back on it. In
desperation, she pressed her hands
on the outside wall, hoping that
somehow his grip would falter.

"Heheheheheheheheh," he continued to laugh.

Daphne continued to thrash her
legs about in an attempt to break
free, but to no avail—his grip was
too strong. As she held onto for
dear life, the wall swayed dramati-
cally every time he pulled, as if it
was ready to come down.

"Come on Buddy, you can't get
me!" she taunted. She braced for
pain as he yanked as hard as he
could. The wood beneath her arms
cracked as she lurched forward,
splinters digging into her skin. The
wall swayed violently as he continued to yank on her. "Come on!"

He yelled as he gave one more violent tug, causing the decaying wall to finally tumble over. He dropped Daphne's leg to protect himself from the falling burnt wood, raising his arms to his face at it impacted him.

While freed from the killer's grasp, Daphne's gambit came at a price. Chunks of the building crashed down on her legs. She winced as the wooden beams dug into her lower extremities.

She struggled to stand up, amazed at her luck that the collapse hadn't crippled her. The walk back to the house was a slow ordeal, with the pain limiting her to a step every few seconds.

"Yeah, sorry coach I can't play the rest of the season," she muttered. "Why? Well it's a funny story, you see this building collapsed on my legs while this axe wielding maniac chased me." She stumbled back into the cottage. "Keys, I need the keys. Where did you throw them you bastard?"

She waddled across the floor towards the back room, where she believed the killer tossed Ritchie's keys. Upon reaching the door she blindly felt the wall before discovering the light switch. A single 40 watt bulb dangled, illuminating the tiny eight by eight foot room. She scanned the floor and was relieved to see them resting against the back wall.

As she leaned over to get them there was a loud thud from the doorway. Startled, she tumbled to the ground.

"Why won't you die?!" she
yelled, whipping around as fast as
her injury allowed.

Pete stood in the doorway.
"Good to see you too hon," he
wheezed, his throat still marked
with the Butcher's handprints.

Daphne collapsed, her back
resting against the wall. She smiled
and began laughing as she held up
the bloody set of keys. "You wanna
get out of here?"

"You have no idea," he said as
he moved towards her.

His progress was interrupted
when a bloody bandaged hand grabbed
his shoulder.

"Pete!" Daphne screamed as the
Butcher plunged his hand through her
boyfriend's chest. She choked on her
breath at the sight of her love's
heart in the evil man's fist.

The maniac shoved the corpse to the ground, sliding his arm back through the hole he'd made in Pete's chest.

Daphne braced herself against the wall to help get off the ground, but her opponent was too quick. He lifted her off of the floor by the throat. She swung a few times as the life choked out of her, but the impact barely drew a reaction from him.

"Hehehehehehehe," the killer laughed as he squeezed his toy tightly.

Daphne stared into the gleeful joy in his eyes brought on by her slow agonizing death. She gasped for air, swinging her arms wildly.

A sharp pain licked her right arm as it clipped something hard. She looked over and saw the knife still embedded in his shoulder. Using every bit of strength she still had, she wrapped her hand around the blade and pulled. As soon as it was free she jabbed it directly into his eye.

The pain forced the behemoth to let go of his prey.

He thrashed about in the tiny room, slamming against the walls.

Daphne scrambled on the floor, narrowly avoiding being crushed beneath a giant's foot. Horrific screams continued from the back room as she stumbled through the house towards the front door.

"No, this ends now," she said, and turned back to the kitchen. She flung open the cabinet doors and grabbed two large moonshine containers before moving back towards her tormenter. The Butcher collapsed onto the floor and took notice that his plaything was still here.

"Hehehehehehehehehe," he laughed and wrapped his hand around the hilt, pulling the blade from its fleshy sheath.

"Yeah you keep laughing," Daphne taunted as she threw the two glass containers in his direction. They landed a couple feet in front of him, shattering upon impact. The liquid streamed into the small room and soaked into his clothes.

"Heheheheheheheheheh," he continued.

Daphne pulled out Cooper's lighter and flicked it on. "Burn mother fucker," she snapped before tossing it.

The metal lighter clanged against the floor, spinning around before settling. The flame quickly spread across the liquid, engulfing the Butcher. He screamed while desperately patting himself down, doing nothing but escalating the blaze. His prey quickly hobbled towards the exit as the shrieks of pain continued.

She reached the van before collapsing on the ground, exhausted from the ordeal. "That's right, burn mother fucker!" she screamed.

Her jovial tone ended when her screams were answered from the house. She tensed up as the flaming Butcher emerged from the doorway, sprinting down the trail towards the lake.

"How are you alive?!?" she screamed.

"How are you alive?!?" She clawed at her face.

"How are you alive?!?"

EPILOGUE

"You're lucky to be alive, you know that?" the nurse asked as she checked Daphne's vitals. "But I wouldn't worry too much, your in- juries should heal in a few weeks and you'll be good as new."

Daphne sat unresponsive, decid- ing it was better to keep quiet than to lay into this sheltered nurse. Physical wounds may heal, but the mental ones that come with watching your friends butchered were going to take a bit longer.

"Ma'am, do you mind if I ask you some questions?" a police de- tective asked from the doorway. "We'd really like to find out what happened up there."

"Sure, come on in," Daphne responded, catching the nurse off guard.

"Glad you aren't mute anymore," she said playfully, prompting a glare from Daphne.

The officer stepped forward. "Daphne, I'm Detective Winston Jones. Can you tell me what happened?"

"My friends and I went up to the lake for the weekend, just to have some fun. Then the first night we were there Buddy Bagwell started killing everyone," she answered.

"Oh honey that's just an urban legend," the nurse blurted out, again drawing her patient's ire.

"Nurse, could you give us a few minutes?" Detective Jones politely asked.

"Okay, if you need anything I'll be right outside," she said before exiting the room. Detective Jones locked the door behind her before moving closely to Daphne.

"Why did you say Buddy Bagwell?" he asked, eyes stern.

Daphne was flustered at his reaction. "Because… because one of my friends told us the story about Camp Barlow."

Jones paled. "What did he look like?"

"He was large, like six and a half feet tall. Over three hundred pounds," she replied.

He swallowed hard. "Did he have burns?"

"He was all bandaged up like he was hurt," she told him.

"Did he have burns?" the Detective demanded.

"I don't know but he does now, because I set his ass on fire!" Daphne snapped.

Jones clenched his jaw. "Is he dead?"

"I don't know. He was running towards the lake the last I saw him." She shook her head.

The Detective paced, disturbed by the news.

"Detective Jones, why are you upset?" Daphne's brow furrowed.

"Because *I'm* the one who found Buddy ten years ago up at that camp," he explained. "*I'm* the one who decided to protect the camp own-ers instead of sending Buddy to jail. And ever since he burned down the Bastrop Asylum last month, *I'm* the one that's been hunting him down."

"No, that can't be." She gasped. "So Buddy Bagwell is real?"

The Detective nodded. "And he's still out there…"

END

www.ingramcontent.com/pod-product-compliance
Lightning Source LLC
Chambersburg PA
CBHW071012180726
48291CB00004B/1423